Biff wanted to help Mum, so
   Mum gave her a job.
'Pick up the apples so I can cut
   the grass,' said Mum.

1

Biff picked up an apple.
'Yuk!' she said.
'Some of the apples are bad.'
She didn't pick up the rotten ones.

Mum made Biff pick up all
   the rotten apples.
'Put them in the box,' said Mum.
'This is a rotten job,' said Biff.

Biff put the box of apples by
   the dustbin.
'Yuk! Rotten apples!' she said.

Kipper was excited.
'Come and see this!' he said.
'What is it?' asked Biff.
'Come and see,' said Kipper.

A man with a horse and cart came
   down the street.
The man stopped outside the house.
'It's Harry Smith,' said Chip.

Everyone liked Harry Smith.
He made people laugh.
He wore a top hat and a red coat.
He sold things from his cart.

Harry Smith rang a bell.
'Come and see!' he said.
'I've got some birds going cheap.'
Biff and Chip laughed.

Mum bought some logs.
The logs were heavy.
Harry Smith helped Mum to
   carry them.

Biff looked at the horse.
'Can we give the horse an apple?'
    she asked.
'Yes,' said Harry Smith.

Biff picked up an apple.
She held it out.
The horse took it with
 its big teeth.

The horse saw the box of apples.
It began to eat them.
'Oh no!' said Biff.
'It's eating all the bad ones.'

Biff told Harry Smith about the horse.
Harry laughed.
'I didn't know she liked
   rotten apples,' he said.

Biff looked in the box.
It was empty.
All the apples had gone.
'What a greedy horse!' said Biff.

The children wanted a ride.
'Jump up!' called Harry Smith.
The children climbed on the cart.
'Hold on!' said Harry.

The horse began to run.
Harry Smith pulled the reins.
'Slow down!' he shouted.
But the horse went faster and faster.

The horse ran down the street.
'Slow down!' shouted Harry Smith.
'Stop!' shouted Mum.
'Help!' shouted the children.

The horse wouldn't stop.
It ran and it ran.
Mum ran after it.
Harry Smith pulled the reins.

It ran into a car park.
'Look out,' shouted Harry Smith.
The horse began to sway.
It made a funny noise.

The horse went slower and slower.
Suddenly, it stopped.
Then it sat down and
    went to sleep.

Harry Smith and the children
    climbed off the cart.
'The horse is drunk,' said Mum.
'Why is it drunk?' asked Biff.

Harry Smith looked at the horse.
'The rotten apples made the
    horse drunk,' he said.
Biff was sorry.

HARRY SMITH
Supplier of garden gnomes to the Duke of York (pub)
ORNAMENTS · FIREWOOD · PEAT · MULCH · COMPOST · ETC ·

Harry Smith laughed.
He didn't mind.
People came to see the horse.
They bought things from the cart.

Harry Smith sold everything.
He gave the children a present.
'Biff's rotten apples did me a
 good turn,' he said.

Printed in Hong Kong